BEFORE THE MOON

THE LUNAR LOVESCAPE PROLOGUES

ESSIE POWERS

CONTENTS

LOUISE

COFFEE AND HOPE

*L*ouise Williams wrestled her gaze away from the man who had just walked in through the doorway of the *Sonic Aromas* café in Shepherd's Bush, London.

She had to stop herself from doing that — *staring*.

Her mother had always chided her about how it was a bad habit; about how it could get her into all sorts of trouble . . . although she never elaborated satisfactorily on just what that 'trouble' might be.

Louise ducked her head and sipped at the foam of the double-shot cappuccino she had ordered. She only realised she draped the tips of her blond hair in the liquid when she heard the grim *drip-drip* of the foam sliding free. She cleaned herself up using the napkin provided with her coffee.

Satisfied that her appearance was at least pass-able, she breathed in the thick, milky scent of the cappuccino, feeling it instantly warm her from within. Her body trembled at the prospect of the caffeine which would soon be coursing through her veins. It faded out all the others sounds of the café: the swirling, steaming espresso machine; the near-constant *tinkle* of coffee spoons against porcelain saucers; the low-level *buzz* of conversation, the sort of sound which seemed impossible to capture under any other circumstances. It was so different from the sound of conversation on public transport, or at the cinema, or in shops. Sometimes, while home in her boxy studio apartment — alone — she would have her earpiece play back the ambient sounds of a café.

Somehow it made her feel *cosier*.

Like she hadn't made an enormous mistake — the *biggest* mistake in all her life — by leaving her hometown of Bristol behind to pitch it all on a shot at the Big City.

Despite having picked out a smart, silky, jet-black trouser suit for her round of job interviews, and despite the fact that she wore it now, she didn't feel like anything but a pretender here. Just *who* did she think she was to arrive here, barely out of her teens, and to be trying to make it in the Adult World . . .

with all these people who had *experience,* and *know-how*; not just wishy-washy *qualifications.*

Maybe it was the nerves — or maybe it was because she simply couldn't help herself — but she tilted her head back once more.

Took in the man who'd just walked in again.

It was the way he walked; how there was a certain *swagger* about him. Louise guessed him to be in his mid-thirties, early-forties at most. He wore a simple — but clearly expensive — white shirt beneath a scarlet, v-necked, cashmere sweater. His trousers were well-tailored — not too-tight fitting as a lot of men around his age were wont to wear.

That scored him points.

Lots of points.

The man reached the barista at the café counter. Although Louise couldn't hear his voice from where she sat, by the window, it meant she could better focus on the subtle movements of his mouth — the way his lips curled around each of the words; treating each one more delicately than the last. When he flipped a casual glance back behind him, Louise ducked back down to her cappuccino. She reached up and touched her earpiece.

The Link informed her that it was going to rain later. She winced at this news, realising that she'd forgotten to bring an umbrella with her today. She *had* wondered why the Link had been nagging at her when she'd left her apartment. If only she'd thought to reach up and touch her earpiece, the Link would've nudged her into remembering the umbrella.

She gazed out the window, and, inevitably, noted the ominous-looking dark clouds clamouring at the horizon. Soon they would dominate the London cityscape. And the fattened raindrops would fall; thick and grim and grey and, well, wet.

Just her luck that she had another two job interviews this afternoon.

Most likely she would arrive looking like a drowned rat.

She turned her attention back into the café, and then, realising she was staring at the man at the counter again, she concentrated on her frothy cappuccino.

To be honest, this really did seem something like an unjustifiable opulence. She hardly had the money to get the bus home, let alone to buy herself a sandwich . . . but, as she'd passed by *Sonic Aromas*, as she'd caught the thick scent wafting out from within, she'd been unable to hold herself back. And so here she was. Sheltering from the coming storm. Filling herself with a warming liquid before she had to face the Big Bad — but especially *cold* — World, all over again.

"Excuse me?"

Louise held herself very still.

A tightness settled across her chest.

Then she glanced up.

It was the man; the one in the scarlet sweater.

He was staring down on her, grinning broadly.

"Uh, sorry," Louise said, quickly glancing around the café, realising that the whole place was just about rammed. She peered down into her cup and quickly realised that only a measly little splash remained in the bottom. She reached for the sensible, beige trench coat which hung off the back of her chair.

Cast a quick — *final* — glance at the man, and then trotted away from him, through the neatly organised tables and chairs to the door.

SINK OR SWIM

*T*he job interviews that afternoon went very badly.

Just as the Link had attempted to advise her, she would've been much better off with an umbrella.

Sopping wet, her hair hanging down in rags, she staggered out of the warm office; what had served as the location for her final interview that day. She made for the nearest bus stop.

When she got back home — or to what qualified as 'home' in this humourless, cold city — the electricity was out.

She knocked on her stand-offish neighbour's door and realised it was only her apartment which was affected. She supposed she should've been thankful that it wasn't the middle of winter; that she most likely wouldn't freeze to death while she slept because of the lack of central heating.

After a series of phone calls to her landlady — and after having got herself successively fobbed off by her landlady's PA, then son, and then *husband* — she decided to give up. In any case, the Link reminded her, she was now two months overdue on her rent.

She was fairly certain that her landlady was avoiding her for as long as she possibly could; hoping that Louise would resolve the unpaid rent without conflict. And, if not, Louise was certain, the landlady would get in touch with the police, and an Eviction Team would show up at her door. More than once in the past week, Louise had woken from nightmares, certain that she could hear the synthesised voices of the Eviction Team droids demanding she leave.

Still wearing the same clothes she had worn that day, she collapsed down onto her mattress. She must've lain there for hours and hours. She thought things over — thought *everything* over . . . and she couldn't help but keep coming back to the same conclusion. That it had been a big mistake —

nothing less than the *Biggest Mistake of her Life* — to come to London and try to make it.

With that conclusion etched across her consciousness, she drifted off to sleep.

END OF HOPE

*T*he next day, after a quick morning visit to the automated drycleaners on the corner, she realised that she had no credits to pay. She returned to her apartment, dressed in the aged, tortoiseshell-green tracksuit she'd bought once upon a time when she'd been on a fitness drive.

Although she wanted nothing more than to slump onto her bed and slip away to sleep — to *forget* about all that'd happened today — she forced herself to the kitchen, to at least see if she could get some sustenance down.

The choices were extremely limited:

Cardboard-tasting cereal, or some even-more-cardboard-tasting crackers.

There was no milk, of course. She hadn't been

able to afford a trip to the shops in over two weeks, and it was looking like she was going to head into a world-record third. If only her parents could see her now.

If only they could see what their daughter was *doing* with her life.

After she'd chomped down on the cardboard-tasting cereal, and because there seemed to be nothing else for her to do, she decided to go for a walk in the nearby park. Once she'd lost herself among the dog walkers and mid-morning runners, things didn't seem to be so bad. She liked to feel as if she was somehow part of a larger fabric, as if she wasn't as alone as she had always thought herself to be. If she could just find one person — a *friend* — someone she could share her experiences with. But — just looking about the faces of those who inhabited the park — she knew that everybody was too *busy* for her . . .

They had better things to do than *cheer her up*.

When she returned to her studio apartment — a room in an old-fashioned, draughty Victorian house — she once more perused the job vacancies on the Link . . . and came away with a Big Fat Zero.

Just like always.

It would always *be this way.*

No escape.

It was almost like an invisible, enormous great pit was opening up around her. And that it was threatening to suck her downward, into the centre of the Earth. That it would smother her until she was dead, and gone. And all she had to do was allow herself to *sink* . . . to fade *away* . . .

She pulled herself back from the brink, almost like she physically reached out for a ledge. She managed to get a hold. To stop herself from tumbling down to her certain death. Determined to get out of her studio apartment — and determined to feel *better* — she dug through her wardrobe, managing, by some miracle, to turn up a pink, toggle-button, satin blouse and a pair of not-too weathered black jeans.

She threw the beige overcoat about her shoulders and shifted out the door.

AIMLESS WANDERING

*L*ouise had no destination in mind, of course. She had only wanted to get free of the stilted air of her studio apartment. And although the London air was hardly what she would call 'fresh', it was a welcome change. It was the change she required.

She stuffed her hands in her overcoat pockets, and, about an hour's walk later, found herself back in Shepherd's Bush; standing on the pavement just outside *Sonic Aromas*. Her whole body went rigid with the thought of the cappuccino she'd supped on the day before. When she checked her bank balance on the Link, wondering if her daily credit limit had been refreshed, she was disappointed.

She couldn't cobble together the credits for so much as a cinnamon stick.

Turning away from the café, and with her weary mind cottoning onto the prospect that she could only return to her apartment now, she heard a voice.

A *familiar* voice.

Or was it just that any voice — any *human* voice — sounded familiar to her?

In the city, she had grown so accustomed to the synthesised tones of droids that she'd almost forgotten humans possessed the ability to speak for themselves.

She looked in the direction of the voice.

And there he stood.

The man from the day earlier.

Although he wore an overcoat — an elegant, charcoal shade — which hung right down to his ankles, she could make out the clothing he wore beneath.

Whereas the day before he had worn the scarlet sweatshirt, he was now wearing a violet one. With the same, sensible, plain, white shirt underneath, the collar sticking up through the v-shaped neck.

"You look like you could do with a good cup of coffee," he said.

Realising he was smiling, Louise couldn't help

but at least *try* to turn back the corners of her own mouth. "I was just . . . *leaving*," she said.

The man pouted. "Come on," he said. "I'm buying."

Louise glanced up the street, as if the city itself was about to offer her some advice. Seeing that there was none, she turned back into the man. "Okay," she replied, "that'd be great."

A CHANCE ENCOUNTER

*L*ouise felt as if she had pins and needles sticking into her skin.

All over her body.

It was the oddest feeling.

She breathed in the thick scent of milk in the air, felt the warming steam against her cheeks, and still tasted the chocolate chunks from the muffin they'd consumed between them.

Several times throughout the conversation, when she'd imagined he — *Alex Barn*, as he'd introduced himself — hadn't been watching, she'd reached up and felt her face. Felt the form of the constant smile which spread her lips. It seemed such a long time since she had allowed herself to smile — to *laugh* — so thoroughly.

'Alex' — not 'Mr Barn', as he had corrected her — had recounted various stories of business meetings gone bad. Louise had no idea that these executives — because that was surely what Alex Barn was — had so much fun.

As the conversation went on, though, Louise couldn't help but feel a sense of guilt growing within her. While Alex had been extremely candid about his own life, and generous in sharing his funny stories, Louise hadn't said hardly *anything* about herself.

To be quite honest, there really weren't that many funny anecdotes to be had.

Not these days.

Right at the point when Louise was certain Alex was going to prod her carefully but firmly for a little personal information, he leaned over the table, and whispered — despite the bristling conversations all around — "Want to know a secret?"

Intrigued by the vaguely naughty, slightly child-like tone, she could do nothing but nod in reply.

Alex spread his arms wide, indicating the café which surrounded him. "This all belongs to the company I work for."

Louise wasn't quite sure what to make of this detail. She supposed that Alex was angling for some kind of shock; that he wanted to make a *splash* . . . but it somehow seemed to square with just who she had already painted him to be.

It didn't come as much of a shock at all.

She turned her attention back onto him.

"And who do you work for?"

"Ah," he replied, and tapped the side of his nose.

"Cocaine dealers?" Louise blurted out, without thinking.

Alex rolled his eyes, smiled slightly. "No, not cocaine dealers . . ."

"Then who?"

Alex seemed almost to lose interest in the conversation. His eyes drifted about the café, settling upon various, apparently random details: a pushchair; a group of three elderly men arguing; a group of girls with asymmetrical hairstyles, more piercings than Louise could count, and a penchant for laughing like drains.

Finally, his gaze returned to Louise. "I think that I'll need something in return for *that* little titbit."

"What?" Louise replied, immediately realising how naïve she sounded.

Alex smiled broadly then sat back in his chair. He folded his arms across his chest, clearly enjoying the whole exchange, and, particularly, the cat-and-mouse game which was unfolding. "A kiss," he stated, clearly, unambiguously.

HOPE FOR THE FUTURE?

*A*lthough it hung over the rest of their meeting, neither of them said anything more about the 'kiss'. It was funny how soon something like that could be apparently forgotten. A beat or so after the silence had descended following the declaration, Alex had broken through it with a brief chuckle, followed by yet another anecdote about his work. And, strangely, and very much *unlike* other anecdotes about work, it actually made her laugh along just as much as Alex.

When Alex used his earpiece to check the Link for the time, he declared that he had to get going. That he had meetings to attend.

Not really knowing what to do, Louise rose up with him.

It was only when the two of them stood outside the café, on the pavement, with the cool breeze wafting up from the Thames, that Louise caught the sensation of prickling pins over the surface of her skin all over again. She knew that this moment had to come about, that they would need to part. That Alex would need to return to his — *surely* — luxury lifestyle filled with excitement and laughter, while Louise would go back to her cold, lonely studio apartment and come to terms with her inevitable exit from the city.

Alex tugged up his overcoat collar, apparently feeling the cold just as much as she did. For some reason that small detail touched her heart . . . it made them feel more *connected*. "So," Alex said, breathing in deeply, and then puffing out gently. "About that *kiss*?"

Louise felt herself blush slightly. It wasn't like her to feel intimidated in the company of men. In fact, she'd always believed it to be one of her greatest strengths that she was willing to stand up and be counted just like anybody else. She didn't want to make excuses in either her life or her career.

She pushed away the sense of anxiety, the warming coffee swilling up through her, and making her feel cosy — almost *at home* — for the first time since she'd arrived to London.

"Will you tell me who you work for?" she said.

Alex smirked. "I'll better *that* . . . I'll give you a job."

It felt as if somebody had punched her square in the solar plexus.

For several seconds, she was simply speechless.

It was like her throat had constricted of its own accord.

"A . . . *'job'* ?" she replied, sure that she was sounding like a complete ditz . . . about as much of a ditz as when she'd implied that Alex worked for coke dealers.

Alex took a step toward her.

She breathed in his sweet, musky scent.

A thousand different worries blazed through her mind.

What if he was married?

What if he was leading her along?

What if he was *crazy*?

What if . . . what if . . .

But, before she could bring any further questions to the surface of her mind, Alex closed the gap. And, before she could do anything to resist, he pressed his lips up against hers.

At first it was soft.

And then it was *hard*.

Passionate.

Louise lost herself to him, and to the moment. She was barely aware as he sheltered her in his arms, as he pulled her into his impossibly warm chest. And she realised how long it had been since she had experienced true *human heat*.

And, in that moment, she vowed never to go as long without it ever again.

Finally, when they broke apart, Alex was grinning from ear to ear.

Louise continued to taste the slight bitterness of the coffee on her tongue — the bitter taste she had tasted on *his* tongue. Her heart was beating wildly — *out of control* — she wondered if it would ever regain its old rhythm . . . if it would ever regain its old *lonely* rhythm.

"We'll speak soon," Alex said, walking away from her, crossing the street.

As he made it to the other side, Louise couldn't help but call out after him. "You never told me what the name of your company is; who you work for."

Alex paused, glanced back over his shoulder, then said, "Humble Associates." With a slight smile, he added, "I'd remember the name, if I were you, otherwise you might not be able to find the offices." He paused for a long moment. "Or *me*."

Alex trod his way up the street.

He had disappeared from sight for a good few moments before she remembered herself; before she caught onto the fact that she was just standing there, not doing anything. As she finally turned and headed in the direction of her studio apartment, she couldn't help but smile.

Life was miserable, but it was surely — *surely* — about to get one hell of a lot better.

ALICIA

MANY MILES BEHIND. LONG
JOURNEY AHEAD.

*A*licia could feel the sweat oozing out of her every pore. The sun was beating down strong, and the seventy to eighty percent humidity made it seem like her brain was swelling up and pushing at the confines of her skull. Over the course of the last hour or so her backpack had seemed to become heavier and heavier; her gait more and more stooped as she struggled with the weight.

And so, with the sea breeze blowing back her hair, and the azure waves filling her vision, she finally relented, allowing the backpack — and *herself* — to drop down onto the fine sands beneath her feet. She somehow summoned the energy to kick off her ragged trainers; and then to peel off her socks and dump them in a pile beside her. She reached back to her aching shoulders, and gave her muscles a much-needed massage. When she had arrived here, to Surat Thani Railway Station in Phunphin, Thailand, several local men had offered to carry her backpack. But she'd turned them all down. Aside from the fact that she'd learned a long time ago, in Backpacker 101, that she was never — *ever* — under any circumstance, to turn her backpack over to a stranger, she had a certain pride in being the one to do all the carrying; all the *legwork*.

To be doing this all on her own.

That said, it would've been nice to have someone with her right now.

Someone with *clever* hands; the sort of hands that *knew* just where to apply pressure.

From a nearby market, she could smell the sweet odour of bananas, and some steam which carried a note of cinnamon. It frustrated Alicia momentarily to be unable to identify the exact food; the exact delicacy that was no doubt being cooked up. Because cooking was her life.

Or at least it had been back home in Wood Dale, Illinois.

Back before she had run away.

Back before she had realised she couldn't live that way any longer; that, no matter how hard she tried, no matter how harshly she scolded herself, she wouldn't be able to hold herself to her family responsibilities. To her dying grandmother. The woman who had been the most important person in her life for longer than she cared to consider.

She reached for the collar of her sleeveless cotton vest and gave it a few tugs with her finger, trying to allow her throat a little extra room for her to breathe. She had toyed with the idea of stripping it off altogether — she had on a sports bra underneath — but the sight of the Buddhist monks, no further than fifty metres away, had prevented her from doing so.

If there was one thing her globe-trotting had taught her, it was that there was a multitude of lifestyles and cultural sensitivities to tolerate and abide by.

It had taken her a few weeks of travelling to get her head properly around the backpackers' creed of 'take only photographs, leave only footprints', but she felt she'd got it down pretty well now.

She made out the sun, caught in its tangerine fireball, and beginning to sink on the horizon. The nights always came quickly here, in the tropics, and she had eased herself into the constant twelve-hour days. Although she never would've believed it back when she'd been a farm girl, and had been required to rise up at five a.m. sharp to go help with the morning milking in the middle of winter, she had become something of a morning person. It was easier to get up with the sun when it rose every day at six. And so it'd come to pass that while her fellow backpackers were sleeping away the effects of the night before — or in some cases fumbling their way to bed in the early-morning light — Alicia would quietly pick her way out of whichever dormitory she happened to be bedded down in and make her way out into the fresh, cool morning air.

She was always the only foreign tourist on the beach at that time. There would, of course, be the local people getting set for the day's work ahead; loading up their motorcycles with vegetables and meat, preparing to make their early-morning deliveries. Now, though, she could make out the first of the foreigners — the men in their early twenties, or in some cases late-teens, wearing shorts and shirts; while the women emerged in floaty summer dresses, concealing the swimming costumes they wore beneath. With their burned skin and their sun-bleached hair, they seemed out of place; as if they didn't *fit* here.

Just like her, she supposed.

As she reclined on her backpack, resting her head, her aching body, she lost herself in the searing, cloudless blue sky. She could just make out the pale silhouette of the full moon; its craters nothing more than indistinct smudges. For a long while, she remained like that, thinking about nothing and everything. It was only when she was interrupted by someone with — what sounded to her ear — an Irish brogue, that she returned to reality.

"I'd take a bitta care if I were you — tends to whip up a chill 'round this time."

Not really wanting to move, but feeling that she should be polite, she shifted her attention onto the speaker. And she took him in.

Tall.

Thin, but not lanky.

He had tight, well-defined biceps and chest muscles, both of which were shown off well by his close-fitting tank top. Like the other foreign men on the beach, he was wearing shorts, with a pair of flip-flops on his feet. And, like the others — *like her* — his skin was tanned, and his hair had been tousled and bleached blond in the strong, tropical sunlight.

What most drew her in were his green eyes.

There was something about them . . . something *wise* about them.

Something which suggested endless depths beneath.

She noted the chilled bottle of beer he held in his hand. He clutched it to the upper portion of his stomach. Because of the humidity, droplets of perspiration rolled down the bottle. The sight only brought home the extreme dryness in her mouth. When was the last time she'd had something to drink?

"Looked like you could use a brew," he said, and then held the beer out toward her.

Something in Alicia urged her to hold back, to retreat into herself. "I'm all right, thanks," she replied, feeling that her American accent was somehow clumsy — *unwieldy* — when placed alongside the man's Irish one.

The man shrugged a shoulder, still extending the beer toward her. "Really," he said, "take me up on the offer. No obligations." He jerked his thumb over his shoulder. "Got places to be, anyhow, need to get ready for work."

" 'Work' ?" Alicia repeated.

"Yeah," he replied. "Just over there."

Alicia followed where the man had indicated. She saw that it was a beach hut consisting of a wooden frame with rushes for a roof. She could already see steam wafting up into the air. She shifted her attention back to the man.

"They give me room and board, plus a little something in the local currency." He reached up and picked at something in his hair. He looked her in the eye then went on, "The main reason I work there, though, is to learn their methods; to learn how to cook like they do." He shrugged. "Kinda like a course where they pay *me* to learn . . ."

Although on any other day Alicia would've been enthralled to hear what the man had to say, her exhaustion was beginning to get the better of her.

"Take the beer," he said, again thrusting it toward her. "If you like, come by a little later and we'll cook you up something." He smiled, showing off rows of even, perfect teeth. "Might even throw in something on the house if you're in luck."

Alicia took the beer from him, and, with that — true to his word — he turned and trod his way across the beach; away from her.

Maybe it was her exhaustion — maybe it was something *else* — but she tracked him all the way to the hut, and watched him disappear within its interior.

Remembering the bottle of beer in her hand, she turned her attention downward, peered in through the neck at the contents. And then brought it up to her lips. Before she knew it, she'd drained the bottle.

A VERITABLE PARADISE

*I*n the end, Alicia didn't take the man up on his offer that evening. She was simply too exhausted. She managed to track down some lodgings — a wooden hut on stilts — where she threw her backpack down before collapsing on the thin mattress which lay on the floor.

When she woke up the next morning, she stepped outside to take in the sunrise. Once she'd got through with rest and recuperation, she flipped through her backpack, finally turning up the purse where she kept her cash. She had made a withdrawal two or three days ago; got her hands on enough funds to make it through the next week or more. It was money she had saved up from working in a bar in Australia. Although the work had been surprisingly mundane and predictable — *drunks were always that way* — the money had got her this far in her globe-trotting. Pretty soon, though, she knew she would have to slow down; that she would need to either get some kind of job or find some other — more economical — way of living.

Actually, thinking about it, what the man had mentioned the night before, about him working at the beach hut restaurant; wouldn't that be the ideal solution?

She could pick up some new, exotic recipes and keep a roof over her head at the same time. And yet, she couldn't help but feel that she might be encroaching on the man. After all, it was his *own* plan. Because, as she had learned throughout her travels, all backpackers — no matter if they travelled alone or in groups — had their *own* journey.

Throughout the day, Alicia walked the beaches. Today, though, she had the good sense to wear a hat so the sun wouldn't make her feel as if she was walking through quicksand. Sooner than she expected, she reached what looked to be the end of the shoreline; marked out with large, slate-grey rocks and bristling trees. Just beyond, she made out the crashing waves. A little way, on the horizon, she could make out bundling, dark clouds looming. She thought she could smell rain in the air too. By the time she had got back to her hut, the light was fading. Along the shore, dim streetlights had blinked on. Improvised, warm orange lightbulbs hung up from the various shacks which lined the beach. Sellers were preparing all manner of terrific-smelling meats and fruits for the consumption of tourists.

She passed them all despite feeling the void in her gut. She had her mind set on a specific place.

When she reached the shack the Irishman had pointed out to her the day before, she was caught up in doubt. There were so many shacks lining the shore that there was no way she could be one-hundred-per-cent certain that this *truly* was the one.

Indeed, when she peered into the interior of the shack, and saw the three local men, sweating profusely as they jabbed and stoked the soaring, exposed flames, she could see no sign of the Irishman. Although the smells were delicious, she turned around and headed back to her hut. She didn't have funds for what she termed 'frivolous spending' . . . and food, more often than not, entered into that category.

She had hardly taken more than three steps away from the hut when she heard the familiar voice.

The *Irishman's* voice.

"Hey! Hey!"

COOKING UP A STORM

*A*licia turned around, feeling utterly lost for a few moments before somehow finding her balance — getting her bearings — once again.

The Irishman was around back, lugging along an assortment of what looked like potatoes in threadbare sacks. He allowed his current load to drop at his feet, taking a moment to steady it against the exterior wall, and then, dusting off his hands, he turned his attention full onto her.

"So," he said, coming closer, "you decided to hang around?"

Alicia managed to get out a slight smile.

And the Irishman, apparently taking just about anything he could get, seized on his opportunity to give her a full-blooded, shit-eating grin. He reached his hand out to her. "Don't think we were intro-duced properly, were we now?"

More dumbstruck than anything else, she took his hand and gave it a friendly squeeze. "No," she replied, "I don't think we were."

"Name's Eng-iss."

" *'Eng-iss'* ?"

"Yeah, that's it," he replied, breaking off their handshake. "Spelled A-E-N-G-U-S. *Aengus.*"

It took her a few more moments to get her head around this, and then she thought she'd finally got it. She managed to regain something of what she'd always believed to be her 'spunk'.

"And what's an Irishman doing this far from the Emerald Isle?"

Aengus gave her a wry smile, and then he extended his index finger, pointing it directly at the tip of her nose and giving it a waggle. "I could very easily ask you the same question, *ma'am.*"

The way he stressed 'ma'am' made Alicia feel as if he thought she was some kind of Southern Belle. She didn't see the point in setting him right. Letting people — *especially men* — know too much about you too soon was a recipe for disaster.

Was that one of those lessons her grandmother had taught her?

Feeling a strange pinching sensation in her gut, she shifted her attention back to Aengus. "The other day," she said, "you insinuated that there might be food — that there might be a free *meal* on the cards."

Aengus flashed his eyebrows. "Oh, did I now?" He reached around and scratched the back of his neck. Then he shifted a glance back to the hut. "I've got another seven of those potato sacks to haul in here. If you give me a hand with them, I'll see what I can do . . ."

Alicia thought on this a moment. She was still aching all over from lugging her backpack the day before. And she had hardly taken it easy on herself today, what with all the walking along the beaches. But that didn't mean she was going to turn down the prospect of a free meal, no matter how slight the possibility.

They got done with the potato-sack lifting within about twenty minutes.

She hadn't realised just how far she would be required to lug the sacks, but it turned out to be quite a way back to the road; to the truck which was parked up there, and to the driver who seemed to take humour from the sight of two foreigners putting their backs into some *real* work.

When Alicia got through with all the lifting, she

felt as if she'd done enough to deserve the free meal which'd been dangled just in front of her nose. But she couldn't help noticing how things had got a lot busier about the shack; how there were now lots of tourists cramming around the façade, jabbering their orders out in loud English with plenty of hand gestures thrown in for good measure.

Aengus gave her a smile which hinted at something like apology, though why he should feel that he had anything to apologise for escaped her. He had a job to do.

To tell the truth, she felt less than useless as she stood on the periphery, feeling as if she was some worthless, passive observer to the frantic activity taking place within the kitchen. She had to admit that she was a little awestruck by the scene within the shack, the constant motion, how Aengus and the three local men who ran the shack ebbed and weaved among one another; at times appearing beneath an elbow or an armpit. A few times she caught an arm shooting over a shoulder, pitching in with a helping hand at something or snatching up some condiment or ingredient.

And then there were the smells.

The thick grease and the buttery, bitingly spicy flavours seemed to twirl through the air, and to jab at the nostrils. As she stood her ground, she began to feel like one of the many stray dogs which plagued the streets, sitting themselves down and watching food preparation and consumption with wide eyes.

After about an hour or so, the crowds began to clear.

Alicia noticed how several fires had sparked up along the beach. And she noted how these were accompanied by the sound of a couple of acoustic guitars. Out-of-tune singing. Some of the tourists splashed about in the shallows of the sea.

With his features now looking a little more drawn, his skin a little slacker, and a pair of dark circles beginning to make themselves noticed beneath his eyes, Aengus emerged from the shack grinning.

Alicia noted how *great* he smelled from the spices and oils he'd been using to cook. Good enough to eat, she might say . . .

It was only when he'd been standing before her for about a minute, attempting to get his breath back, that a look of shock passed over his face. He slapped his forehead like some cartoon character. "*Shit!*" he said. "I totally forgot."

Alicia couldn't help but enjoy the slight slip of Aengus's otherwise firm and sure outlook; the version of himself he presented to the world. In that moment, as he'd reacted purely, he'd seemed just like some adolescent; showing off his *boyish* charm.

Almost instantly, he produced a paper plate from within. Just like one of the many they had handed out to the paying tourists. Despite her hunger, Alicia couldn't bring herself to do anything but fully appreciate the cuisine she held before her.

Steamed rice.

Some kind of leaves — she believed them to be known as *pegagan* from what she had garnered so far during her travels.

Onions.

Some shoots she couldn't quite think to identify.

. . . And then — with the delicious odours now overwhelming her — her patience dissolved.

She seized the spoon which'd been provided and began to scoop into the rice.

After she'd pushed in the first mouthful, she glanced around, realising that Aengus, too, had produced his own plate. And that he was also hungrily devouring its contents. He paused for a moment, though. He looked up at her and declared, "*Nasi ulam.*"

"Huh?"

"It's a type of *Ahan Phak Tai*. Cuisine from the region."

"Oh," Alicia replied, feeling that she was getting free education to go with the free food.

This really was turning out to be a valuable evening.

NIGHTLY WONDERS

*T*here apparently not being anything else for them to talk about, they finished up their *Nasi ulam* in silence. When they'd finished, Aengus offered her another serving, but she turned him down. It was always surprising just how quickly she became full after a long day without eating. She did, however, accept the offer of a beer and a moonlight walk along the shore.

As she strode alongside him, she couldn't help but notice her heart beating a little steadier than usual. She could feel as if the fatigue which held her body in a vice-like grip was easing off somewhat. As if the alcohol was doing its work.

They passed by the dozens of campfires burning on the beach, past the strumming would-be troubadours, and beyond the couples splashing about in the surf. It was a clear night and the sky was dotted with bright stars. The moon was full and it shed its whispering, white light over them.

When they reached the end of the beach, Alicia was stuck for what she should do. Of course she had had romances on her trip. They had always been sudden, passionate events. And they would end just as quickly as they began.

But, somehow, being here with Aengus, walking along the beach with him, she caught the feeling that this time things would be different.

That this wasn't a romance like any of the others.

"How long've you been running?"

"Hmm?" Alicia said, having drifted off into something like a doze.

However, when the question sunk home, she felt her senses suddenly pull tight. Her heart rapped faster against her throat, and she felt herself withdrawing.

Aengus shrugged. "Two years, seven months and eighteen days."

To begin with his stone-faced expression took her off guard.

He was suddenly so serious.

But — just when she began to feel concerned — he broke into a grin.

He turned back to her and said, "I guess we all have our secrets, huh? We all have our past *demons* . . ."

Alicia met his eye briefly, matched his smile, and then turned her attention back out ahead of them. "I just needed a change," she said. "A chance to be myself."

"Is that where the whole cooking thing comes from, then? Is that what you found when you looked within yourself?"

She turned into him, narrowing her eyes for a fraction of a second.

He let out a chuckle, then said, "It's fairly obvious when I come across someone with culinary flare. They don't scoff food down the second you serve it to them. They take their time, appreciating every last detail."

She thought on this a moment, remarking to herself that Aengus was more perceptive than she had originally pinned him to be. What that meant, in real terms, she wasn't sure she could say.

She switched her attention to his first question, realising that he was probably expecting an answer. "No," she said, "actually my cooking — my 'flare' for cooking — comes from my grandmother . . . not from myself."

"Ah," he replied, turning his attention back front and centre; to the path they trod along the shore, among the calm, lapping waves washing into the beach. He was quiet for another few moments before he slipped her a sidelong glance. "And so, if you already *found* what you're looking for then why'd you bother leaving home to keep on looking?"

A tightness stretched across Alicia's chest.

Her stomach dipped.

She took a sharp breath.

And she realised she was going to tell him the truth.

"I . . ." she began, ". . . couldn't *cope* with things . . . with *how* things were going . . . with how things *were* . . ."

Another moment of silence passed and then he said, "Well that's awfully specific."

Against all odds — against the sadness which she felt at leaving her grandmother and her *family* behind — she snorted a laugh.

Finally, when she realised that now *was* the time for her to speak to someone — that now *was* the time for her to come clean — she said, "I couldn't cope with her getting ill; I couldn't cope with being around her while she . . ." here something caught in her throat, but she kept going ". . . while she was *dying*."

Another silence settled in over them.

The waves washed in and out, and the distant sound of strumming guitars provided an ethereal backdrop. Having shucked her flip-flops a while back, she savoured the feeling of walking upon the sand, feeling it rubbing against the soles of her feet. It was then, as they were nearing the end of the beach, that she felt Aengus's hand brush her own. Almost as if she was still some naïve farm girl, she flinched at his touch.

But he was firm, gentle.

His fingers wrapped around hers.

Then squeezed.

She waited a heartbeat.

And then squeezed back.

It was then that she felt herself turning into him.

And him turning into *her*.

When he planted his lips on hers, it was almost as if she might finally melt in the humid air. It felt as if warmth pressed in on all sides. She acted on instinct, reaching out and running her hands up his muscular back, and to his shoulders. She finally settled for combing her hands through his tangled hair.

She peered into his never-ending, glittering emerald eyes.

When they did break apart, it was her who made a point of being the next to speak. "I'd like to stay," she said. "At least for a while."

She turned her gaze back across the beach — across the *gorgeous* backdrop. And then she looked into his eyes. "There're things that I can learn here — there are things that I can learn from *you*."

Aengus held himself very still. His seriousness had made something of a return. His stone-faced expression had come back. He released a long exhale and then gazed off into the distance; out across the beach. When he did turn back into her, he was smiling again. He seemed to give off a warmth. "You know," he said, "I think you have some things to teach me too." He paused, as if thinking over his next words carefully. "We really could be a great team."

And as they headed back along the beach, she had thoughts of the mattress, and her backpack she had left within the hut. She could hardly think of a more comfortable — more *homey* — place to bed down.

Even if it was only for a couple of months.

LAN

A SUNNY DAY IN SPAIN

*H*igh above — set against the searing, azure sky — the sun beat down; its heat bringing up quivering rays from the cobblestones in the streets far below. Lan Niu leaned up against the white-painted concrete of the balcony. It, too, was baking-hot. She had often wondered whether it was truly possible to fry an egg on the ground . . . if she'd had one right now, then she might just have given it a go.

Her whole body seemed ready to boil in the black jumpsuit she wore. She decided that whoever had thought out how they would dress today was some sort of masochist. That factor aside, it had been an impractical decision too . . . because it made it difficult to concentrate. And if it was *this* unbearable early in the morning then who was to say how it would be in around an hour's time, when the sun *really* hit?

As a bead of sweat ran down the side of Lan's face, she thought back to her briefing for the day. The current job she was working took place in the town of Buñol, Spain. More or less the first thing she'd done when she'd arrived at Barajas airport in Madrid was sign on to work for a security agency.

It was what she did best.

A hired gun.

Somehow, in the ten years since she'd been gone from her home in Shanghai, she'd ended up travelling just about everywhere. And the security work had been a means to pay her expenses. She guessed that if she'd been a man she could've called herself a 'drifter'; though, being a woman, and it not being as in vogue for a women to go through with the same lifestyle, she really had no idea *what* to call herself. So she just called herself a 'security guard'. That job title seemed to satisfy border officers sufficiently, at least.

Today was the festival known as *La Tomatina*.

As Lan had drawn from her boss's explanation of the event, it was a celebration which involved all the townspeople — and the many tourists who turned up for the fun — throwing tomatoes at one another.

Lan, though, would be an arm's length from the festivities.

She was on duty.

Her task today was to protect the young offspring of some local bigwig.

For the job, she had been given access to a constantly updating set of coordinates for the person she was supposed to protect. That had been patched into her connection to the Link so that she might be able to keep track of them. There was an abridged profile, too. Lan knew, from her experience with such jobs, that those who employed the services of security agencies were not all that interested in giving too much information away about them-selves; lest they become targets. She had learned that most security agencies barely had a better reputation than the thieves, kidnappers and extortionists, they were supposed to protect their clients from. From the abridged profile which showed in her HUD, she saw that it was a young woman; perhaps in her early twenties . . . at least five years younger than Lan; maybe even younger. She had that frail body shape so many women seemed to strive for.

Lan actually made a point of keeping herself

fairly *spindly-looking*, despite her proficiency with weights and cardio. From her experience it was an attractive quality for clients to have a femme fatale at hand; able to ease their enemies into a false sense of security. Right now, though, there wasn't all that much surreptitious about Lan. She was dressed in a black jumpsuit, and anyone with more than a passing glance could tell that the bulge down at her right thigh wasn't just the baggy quality of the clothing she wore. If Lan allowed them to get close enough, they would see that she was in fact packing a very capable — *very deadly* — laser blaster.

Good thing she never allowed *anyone* to get close . . .

She glanced across to the next rooftop; saw another member of her team there. Looking *equally* ridiculous — not to mention *conspicuous* — in his black jumpsuit.

Sometimes Lan couldn't help but internally criticise whichever boss she happened to be working with. During her time working security, she had learned one thing about organisations; it was that — more often than not — they ended up being run by whoever happened to hang around for the longest period of time. And, in Lan's opinion at least, longevity was a much overrated attribute when going about selecting management candidates.

Then again, she wasn't about to change that.

Her itchy feet wouldn't allow her.

With a slight sigh at the state of the world — not to mention her role in it — she shifted her attention to the task stretching out ahead.

It was going to be a long day.

TURNING UP THE TEMPERATURE

*T*he actual crowds began to arrive at around nine a.m., and by ten they were positively heaving. Being the diligent little worker that she was, Lan kept an eye firmly fixed on the task at hand; at looking after the young lady.

According to the coordinates at her disposal, she saw that the woman was moving along the cobblestones four or five streets away. When she glanced up, she saw that another of her colleagues held her in firm visual range. Lan tended to tune in and out of the radio gossip which passed between her colleagues — mostly because it was in Spanish: a language which she was still in the early stages of mastering; she could just about stretch to *Hola* and *Gracias*.

She turned her attention onto the scenery surrounding her, thinking about how — back when she'd been a little girl — she would've swooned, or something, at having the opportunity to visit Europe.

Now, though, the intensely *foreign* rooftops, and other assorted architecture — the bright and cheerful amber-and-red flags which fluttered in the breeze — seemed almost a façade. What she'd learned over the past few years of living alone — of *being alone* — was that human civilisation was united in its uniformity.

Realising that she should probably turn her mind to task, she went about subtly inspecting her laser blaster.

"*¿Hola?*"

Lan startled at the sound.

She turned.

Saw that she was staring back at one of her colleagues.

He wore the same black overalls as the rest.

Lan was frozen for several moments, trying to find something — *anything* — which she might be able to summon by way of a reply. She guessed that she wanted to say something snarky; something along the lines of *Shouldn't you be doing your job?* but her rudimentary local language skills wouldn't allow her this. So she just continued to stare. And it took her only a couple of moments to realise that she wasn't staring at him out of some sort of outrage; that she was staring at him, because, well, there was really no way for her to hide it . . . he was *gorgeous*.

She took in his olive skin, and his walnut eyes, and the sculpted, square jaw which seemed such a distinct feature of Europeans. It was strange; there were not many moments when Lan felt something like intimidation creep into her character — when she felt as if she might be in danger of being over-powered — but now was one of those times.

Her heart beat against her ribs.

And a refreshing, cold flush ran through her blood.

The man smiled at her. "You look *hot*," he said, in English. "Where you from?"

Lan took a moment to compose herself before replying. "Shanghai," she said, and then, as if he couldn't work it out for himself, added, "*China*."

"Ah, *China*." There was a hop to the man's voice; as if there was some sort of humour about her country of origin.

A silence formed between the two of them, and Lan felt herself becoming increasingly uncomfortable. She wondered what this man was doing here — what he was doing here with *her* . . . didn't they have a job to do? They couldn't *afford* to be distracted.

"You, ah . . ." the man continued, in slightly broken English. "You stay" — he pointed off across the rooftops, into the distance — "in *Valencia*."

When he spoke the 'c' of Valencia, it was like an 's' sound in English.

It sounded a little like one of the English instructors Lan had had back in school. He had had a lisp and every one of his s's had come out as more of a 'th'. It had taken Lan a long while to adapt and model her own English accordingly so that she didn't sound like she had a speech impediment when she herself spoke.

She glanced back into the man's eyes. "Yes, I'm staying in Valencia."

The man widened his eyes in some sort of mock surprise, or maybe it was genuine enthusiasm. Despite his somewhat wild expressions, Lan couldn't help but find herself imagining — in vivid detail — just how he must look beneath his jumpsuit.

"This is your first time . . ." the man continued. "*Here* . . . in *Ess-spain?*"

Lan held herself still. She was half conscious of the location of the lady they were supposed to be monitoring. She knew that she was just a street over now. When she cast a quick glance about, she saw that twice the amount of people now crowded the streets than had done so before. They were closing in on the most dangerous time.

"Yes," she replied, finally. "It's my first time in Spain."

As if Lan was a mere tourist — and she wasn't packing a laser blaster strapped to her thigh; beneath her overalls — the man pointed down at the crowds, then said, "The event it starts *soon* ..."

"Uh-huh," Lan replied, doing her best *not* to shoot him sidelong glances; trying *not* to take gratuitous looks at his body.

Sure enough, she took in the crowds as they filtered through the streets.

All of them — almost without exception — looked as if they were dressed for a day at the beach. The men wore shorts and t-shirts; some of them going bare-chested. The women, meanwhile, had on skimpy clothing, exposing their shoulders to the increasingly fierce sunlight.

Lan had never quite understood the obsession with getting a 'sun tan'.

From what she'd gathered from the many tourists she'd witnessed in around Spain so far, she believed it to be a kind of single-minded obsession with turning their skin a golden brown.

She switched her attention back to the Link.

To the coordinates of the girl they were supposed to protect.

She was drawing near.

Almost on the same street now.

Somehow being able to flip a switch in her mind — to turn her focus to the task at hand; away from the, admittedly *fine*, specimen beside her.

"Come on," she said, stepping away from the edge of the balcony. "We need to get down to street level."

IN THE THICK OF IT

*O*nce at 'street level', Lan had turned her thoughts entirely to the task at hand . . . or at least she believed she'd done so; she couldn't help but be aware of the man nearby . . . she did her best to avoid looking at him directly. That seemed to be the best option.

She felt suddenly overwhelmed by the crowds passing her by; the people streaming past, all of them in their beach-day wear. She was bumped into more than a few times, and she made an effort to apologise, though it didn't seem to make much difference. The people kept on walking; wrapped up in whatever conversations they were having.

It felt almost like Lan was invisible . . . and yet, at

the same time, as if she was standing out more than anybody else in her jet-black jumpsuit.

She became somewhat paranoid about the blaster down at her thigh; that someone might make a grab for it; that she might have it snatched off her. Although nothing of the kind had ever befallen her on any job she had undertaken, it was one of those wake-up-in-the-middle-of-the-night-in-a-cold-sweat type of dreams.

"This way," the man said, speaking incredibly close to her ear.

Close enough that Lan felt his warm breath.

And she smelled the slight scent of basil and mint which hung there.

He touched her gently on the shoulder as he brushed past, and they continued on through the constantly filling streets; losing themselves among the crowds.

The streets soon opened out into a large square — a *plaza*. Up ahead, she saw several trucks, all of them loaded with tomatoes. Her mind stretched. She glanced about, to her surroundings. Again becoming paranoid.

Her HUD informed her that their client was nearby.

Separated from Lan, and the hunk who was accompanying her, by about a dozen people.

. . . Even as she thought the word, Lan scolded herself.

There was a thick, uncrossable line between work and pleasure.

And she was *very much* on the 'work' side of the line at present.

Right then, he drew up close to her again.

Impossibly close.

And he spoke in her ear.

"My name is *Felipe*. I am very pleased to meet you."

Lan resisted for the longest time. Focusing her attention on the crowds spread out before her. And then, right at the last, she turned to him. "My name's Lan," she said. "Lan *Niu*."

The man — *Felipe* — parted his beautiful lips to say something else, but if he managed to get out any sound then it was completely drowned out by the *roar* which spread across the crowd.

Lan shifted her attention, seeing that the trucks were decanting their load of tomatoes to the waiting people in the square. She watched on as they snatched up tomatoes by the handful. Tomatoes began to hail through the air.

Lan had read ahead of this celebration that it was a regulation that the tomatoes needed to be squashed before being thrown, and, indeed, the majority of the tomatoes being hurled through the air had already been reduced to mulch. The first fragments began to fall upon Lan in a thick paste.

She was aware of clumps becoming caught in her hair.

Before she had entirely got her head around the situation, she found herself becoming covered in the tomatoes. She had to squint to make out anything through the constant hail. Her HUD was affected, too. It gave only the vague, silvery outline of the client they were supposed to protect . . . their client, who, Lan saw, was currently crouched down, apparently — *sensibly* — avoiding the worst of the fire.

Lan felt Felipe's strong grip on her forearm. He tugged her suddenly to one side. With several questions on her lips — not to mention *invective* — she witnessed a huge clump of tomatoes flop over their heads and land with a moist, stomach-churning *squelch* behind them on the cobblestones. When she turned her attention back to Felipe, she saw that he was smiling widely, seemingly pleased with the heroics he had exhibited. He continued to grip her tightly. And, strangely enough, she couldn't find it within herself to tell him to let her go.

For the longest time, she found herself lost in his eyes — in those gorgeous *walnut* eyes.

Her heart skipped several beats.

And his lips drew her attention.

They seemed so full; so *kissable* . . .

An alert ran through her earpiece.

Acting on instinct, because it seemed rational thought had long ago deserted her, she reached up and stuck her finger into her ear so she could better make out the message.

An issue with their client.

With the young woman they were here to protect.

When Lan rose her head, she saw, indeed, that the silvery, shadowy silhouette on her HUD was lying on the ground, amongst the cobblestones. She slipped Felipe a sidelong glance, seeing that he — *too* — was focused on the spot.

He had received the same alert.

Heart bouncing at the back of her mouth, Lan rose to her feet, only to be knocked down by another hailstorm of tomatoes. She managed to block the barrage by holding her arm up to cover her eyes. When she looked to Felipe, she saw that he was experiencing the same difficulties; that he was hardly able to stand up straight.

Another alert sounded in Lan's earpiece.

This time it was more urgent.

A call to *action* rather than a call to be *vigilant*.

She was to get hold of the girl . . . to bring her to safety.

Sure enough, in between the constant storm of tomatoes, she made out the silvery silhouette on her HUD; the girl still lying on the cobblestones assuming a lifeless posture. Lan pressed herself onward, determined to reach her.

One of the members of the crowd butted into her from the side.

Lan had only a second to catch sight of them.

And to see the laser-cutter they held in their hand.

It was a device most used in industry; anything from breaking the tape on tightly wrapped packages to slicing clean through a sizeable brick wall.

Of course, by extension, it would make short work of human skin.

Of human *bone*.

Realising the threat which faced them — and that it was *urgent* — Lan forgot the tomatoes being flung around her; zigzagging through it all.

Several times, she found the going easier when she dropped down to about waist height. When she could bundle her way through the bodies.

When another alert sounded in her earpiece, her heart stuck harder still.

She saw the man with the laser-cutter, and, realising that he was now within only a few steps of the client, lying sprawled on the cobblestones, she decided she needed to act.

She reached down into her jumpsuit, feeling for the blaster strapped to her thigh, nestled in its holster. She slipped it out, and, with a well-practised action, flipped it onto auto-charge.

She delayed taking the shot for as long as she dared.

Although she had set the pistol to STUN, she didn't want to go around stunning innocent bystanders. She had to admit that she wasn't all that well acquainted with just how the local laws treated such attacks. But her employer would protect her against all legitimately taken-down threats. And this man with the laser-cutter seemed like a legitimate threat, if nothing else.

She lined up the shot through the sight.

Drew in a deep breath down to her stomach.

Then squeezed the trigger.

THWARTED

*T*he reaction around Lan was immediate.

People screamed.

Tomato-throwing ceased almost straight away.

Crowds tumbled back from the person Lan had downed with her shot.

It was then, with space opening out ahead, that Lan could finally bring the client within direct visual range. She was no longer spread-eagled on the cobblestones — a sitting duck for the man with the laser cutter. Apparently roused by the crowd's reaction, she was now propped up on her knees, looking about, clearly beleaguered by the ensuing events.

Lan acted quickly.

She trod over the body of the individual she'd stunned, and to the client.

She took her gently — *but firmly* — by the arm.

And she led her off toward the edge of the plaza . . . on the heels of the rapidly departing crowd, all of them caked with tomato skins and juice.

Lan only came to a halt when she had reached one of the Safe Points as marked on her HUD; a spot which happened to be down a nearby alleyway.

The client was breathing rapidly, but seemed otherwise unharmed.

It was then that Lan realised Felipe was with her too . . . that he had followed them away from the plaza. Even despite the situation — despite the constantly diminishing crowds; and the sense of panic — Lan felt an enormous sense of calm.

She had taken care of the infraction.

And she had neutralised the threat.

While Lan set about reassuring the girl — seeing that she apparently understood English — Felipe worked on communicating with the rest of the guards present; informing them of the threat, and that it had been taken care of. When he was through with his communications, he came over to Lan and the girl, and, with a slight smile, said, "A good job."

Lan couldn't quite bring herself to tear her eyes from his.

Almost as if he was sucking her in with his gaze.

IN THE AFTERMATH

*L*ater in the evening, the town of Buñol was deserted.

The crowds had long ago departed.

The event called off in the middle of its celebration.

Because of the laser blast.

Because of the shot which Lan had taken . . . the shot which she'd *had* to take.

Soon after the girl had been turned into the care of other guards — and the potential attacker had been apprehended — Felipe and Lan were debriefed.

Although neither of them was given instructions on what their next task should be, Lan implied that they were to be allowed a brief respite from their work; that they would be allowed to let down their hair for a day or so. And, well, if there was one thing which Lan was determined to do, it was let down her hair.

Local people emerged from their houses; the façades of which were covered with tomato residue. They bore brooms and buckets of water to help wash away the tomato skins which lined the cobblestones. Lan and Felipe walked between them all.

Lan herself felt strange to be walking through all of this abridged pandemonium in her jumpsuit, so she could only imagine what the local people must think of the sight of them.

Not that Lan really cared all that much.

Soon she would be gone.

Allocated far from this place.

Most likely, she would never return to Buñol.

When the two of them reached the main square, Lan realised that they were completely alone. That what had once been an area packed with people — all of them jostling to grab fistfuls of tomatoes off the arriving trucks — was now deserted.

It felt somewhat eerie.

At this time in the day — now late afternoon — Lan could feel the cool breeze floating off the surface of the nearby lake. She stared out across the square and wondered if this was something like the world would feel if it was empty of human beings.

Except for herself and Felipe, of course.

On impulse, she turned to him.

He met her eye.

The charge which'd built between them all day finally reached its climax.

Its attraction was impossible to resist.

Lan felt herself slowly being drawn into him.

And he was being drawn into *her*.

When their lips first touched, Lan's heart dipped right down to the pit of her gut. She thought she might collapse from the lightest of pressures against her lips.

She reached out, pressed her palms up against Felipe's chest.

Felt his *hard* pectoral muscles.

When Lan was unsure she would be able to draw breath again, she leaned back from Felipe, once again finding herself locked in his gaze.

"We have a good time," he said.

Lan analysed his words.

It was obvious what he meant despite his broken, accented English.

And, to be honest, she couldn't help but agree.

KYRA

COMMITTED TO THE CAUSE

*K*yra Singh felt the first flush of the New Delhi sun sear her temples. It summoned a single bead of sweat from her forehead, which subsequently rolled down her face. Her whole body ached. She had been up almost all night . . . but — as she had learned years earlier — sleep wasn't a highly valued commodity in journalism. She had all the time in the world to sleep once she had retired. One of her previous editor's sayings had gone something along those lines.

She blamed her sleep-deprived state for having decided to pull on the thick, black fleece she was now wearing. Deciding that enough was enough — and already beginning to feel the sweat rolling down her back — she unzipped and tied it about the waist of her jeans. She was *glad* that she had gone with rugged footwear — a solid pair of hardened walking boots — the terrain here was somewhat uneven, to say the least.

She eyed the railway spread out before her, missing several wooden sleepers.

It was almost completely dilapidated.

She had been contracted for this job by a media outlet specialising in railways . . . in *everything* to do with railways. The outlet was determined to do nothing less than document each and every last scrap of track on the face of the Earth. Kyra would only play a small part in that grand ambition.

It was when she checked the time on the Link — only barely functioning this far out of the city — that she realised it was already well past nine o' clock in the morning. She had scheduled the photographer to arrive at nine o'clock on the dot. If there was something which bothered her more than tardiness, it was *tardiness* when she'd had to get up early herself.

She'd managed to get here on time.

Why couldn't others do the same?

As she continued to take in the scene spread out before her — the sun rising up behind the tower blocks, like some all-powerful, golden god — she heard footsteps on the rocks which were scattered beneath the rails. She turned to look.

Saw that there was a man approaching.

And . . . well, there was no other way to put it . . . *what* a man!

He wore a pair of waterproof trousers — the kind which might've been favoured by military; or by outdoorsmen. He had a large, well-muscled frame which showed in the way he walked. She could easily make out his rippling biceps for the simple fact that he wore a tight sleeveless vest . . . apparently glad to have the opportunity of showing them off to whoever might be interested. His dark hair hung in casual curtains, bouncing off his forehead, gleaming with a layer of sweat in the early-morning sun. She took in the bag which hung casually off his shoulder. And which bounced against his side as he trod closer to her. As he came nearer still, she was able to take stock of his black — *black* — eyes. They seemed to prod and poke at her . . . testing her as if she was a hunk of meat. She would need to watch herself with *this* one.

When she was close enough to make herself heard, she made sure that the first words out of her mouth were ones of reprimand. "You took your time," she said, addressing him in Hindi.

The man — the *photographer* . . . the hunk — gave her the merest outline of a smile; a smile which showed that he hoped to get his way with his looks, with his appearance, whenever he could manage it. Kyra knew *all about* this type.

How they would get ahead with winks, and smirks, and *lingering* gazes . . .

Well, she knew better. She wouldn't allow him to get to her as he had surely got to many others. With that resolution firmly fixed in her mind, the man held out his hand. "Panchika," he said. "But everyone calls me *Pan*."

Kyra held his stare for a second longer than was necessary, and she was sure to give him a *limp-wristed* handshake. She knew that if she gave him an inch, this 'Panchika' was the type who would take a *mile*. It was hard enough for a woman in the male-dominated arena of journalism — all that ego; all that *testosterone* — that simple kindness was a virtue which she could ill afford.

"Kyra," she replied, peeling her hand free of his grip then turning around to absorb the scene which surrounded her. She gave a sigh, making sure that he knew her feelings well.

Making sure that he *understood* that he was wasting her time.

She had been wondering about taking a photo-journalism course . . . about getting her skills up to a professional standard . . . that would surely solve *problems* such as this one.

How difficult could it be to take some pictures?

"I was thinking we would begin with some wide-angled shots," Kyra said.

She had already taken several steps away from him — expecting that he would follow, like a faithful dog. However, when she turned back, she saw that he was still standing in the same spot. He was squinting at something in the bushes.

Kyra resisted the urge to call out. She wasn't going to lose face, or her temper, with someone who was obviously so keen to get on her nerves in any way they possibly could.

She simply stood her ground, exercising her patience.

Waiting for him to snap to attention.

Finally, he did.

He turned to her.

Looked in her direction.

"I . . . it's just," he said. "There's something there. Something in the bushes."

Kyra resisted the urge to sigh. She wouldn't give him the *satisfaction*. She trod back toward him, at least keeping her mind open to the possibility that this wouldn't be some kind of a windup, although she was fairly certain that was *exactly* what it would be.

Standing beside the man — *Panchika* — she breathed in his warm, fruity scent.

It reminded her of hazelnuts and apples, or something similar.

Despite her best efforts, she found herself wondering what the name of the fragrance he used might be. He *was* using an out-of-the-bottle fragrance, wasn't he? She could hardly bring herself to imagine that he *naturally* smelled this way.

Finally, she got a hold on herself.

Managed to *shut up* those thoughts.

She had work to do.

It was time for her to be a *pro* . . . not to act like some giddy schoolgirl.

Before she got the chance to see what it was Panchika drew her attention toward, he was off; crunching his way through the foliage. Kyra had little choice but to follow. Or else she risked ending up with a piece devoid of photographs or video.

A big *no-no* in the modern age.

She went after him.

Vaguely wondering what she'd done to deserve this.

SURPRISES IN STRANGE PLACES

*T*he child's cries split the air.

They sent a shudder down Kyra's spine.

And twisted her gut.

All previous thoughts — that animosity; because in what other way could she term her opinions about Panchika? — were gone now.

It took all her focus to absorb the sight which stood before her.

The baby. No older than a few weeks.

It lay in a wicker basket.

A blanket tucked up to its chin.

Its tiny, balled-up fists had thrust free and pounded furiously.

Panchika looked back at her with something of a

mixture between fear and concern sketched across his face. As he spoke, he clutched his camera bag close to his hip as if it was some sort of comfort blanket. As if it might have some sort of quality which would prevent this scene from affecting him on an emotional level.

"No one around," he said.

Kyra looked about.

Saw that he spoke truthfully.

They were alone.

A good way off on the outskirts of the city.

To tell the truth, this area was supposedly restricted, but Kyra had used a little journalistic licence to slip through the holes of several chain-link fences which surrounded the railway tracks. It appeared that Panchika had done the same. The authorities kept a close track of people entering and exiting here . . . not to mention those who might choose to make this their home.

This wasn't a mistake.

Someone had brought this baby here on purpose.

So that they could leave it behind.

So that it would be found.

"What should we do?" Panchika said, looking at her.

"I . . ." Kyra started, and then found her attention

caught by the baby's big, beautiful, round eyes. She found herself staring into those eyes. Although she knew it to be impossible — with the baby not being older than a few months — she thought it was communicating with her. That it was trying to get some message through.

Just what exactly that message was Kyra couldn't say.

She looked to Panchika. "We . . . can't leave it here, can we?"

Panchika turned back to the baby, as if he needed to take in the sight again before deciding. Or as if he needed to remind himself that this was really happening. When he turned back to Kyra, he was smiling wildly. And there was something of a twinkle — a warmth — in his eye. "No," he said. "Of course we can't."

Despite herself — despite telling herself that she needed to be professional; and that all her relationships at work needed to be treated as such — she felt a gooey warmth rising up into her chest.

And she became a touch giddy for a second.

RESCUE OPERATION

*K*yra had parked her car up outside a house. She had paid a couple of kids to keep a watch on it. When she turned the corner, leading the way before Panchika and the baby he carried — still in its wicker basket — they immediately slipped off the dilapidated brick wall they were reposing on. Snapping to attention like a pair of overeager soldiers.

Kyra jabbed the fob and her car's hazard lights blinked, announcing that the locks were now disengaged. The boys who had looked over the car, in turn, went to the doors and opened them up.

As Kyra was about to slide into the driver's seat, with Panchika making a move to slip into the passenger side — the baby still gathered in his hold

— a thought struck her. "Your car?" she asked. "Would you like to follow me?"

Panchika shook his head, smiling lightly. "I came on the bus."

The bus, Kyra thought to herself. And she couldn't help but consider whether or not this might be some sort of a *humble* act . . . as if Panchika was trying to show himself to be a salt-of-the-Earth type which Kyra had already decided — by his clothing, his poise, his *job* — that he certainly wasn't. Her softening attitude toward him became a little more rigid. She reminded herself to stay on her guard. She wouldn't be made a fool of . . . not *again*.

She said nothing more.

This was hardly the place or time.

As she pulled out of the parking space, she tossed a few coins to the boys who had attended her. From their nimble catching ability, she supposed that they must pass the time brushing up on their cricket skills.

She left them in her dust, swinging the car onto the dirt road.

Wrestling to keep the backend from sliding out of control.

REFUGE SOUGHT

*I*t was around midday by the time they had got back into the hustle and bustle of New Delhi. Kyra wrestled with the wheel, keeping the trajectory of the car from flying into the path of a rickshaw, or any one of the various motorbikes, bicycles or taxis which seemed to constantly stray across their path. She was following the directions which Panchika gave her. She decided against asking him directly where they were going — deciding that he surely had a much better idea of what to do with this baby than she did. Kyra had read stories about this happening to people — about them uncovering an abandoned child — but she had never expected it to happen to her.

Finally, Panchika instructed her to pull up

outside a white building. The entrance was strewn with vendors of all kinds. Employing her usual strategy, Kyra chose the most trustworthy-looking of the street children which approached her car door. And she handed over some spare change to him, promising that there would be more if her car was unblemished when she returned.

Without a word to her, Panchika passed through the crowd, which parted to allow him through with the baby in his arms. Kyra trailed in his wake, feeling dizzier still at the course of events which'd transpired. Her sleep-deprived state had everything to do with it; her brain was hardly firing on all cylinders. And she had thought this would be such a simple story. She had thought she would be done before midday . . . as long as everything went according to plan.

But — as had transpired — nothing had gone according to plan . . .

Kyra immediately noted the many women — all of them wearing saris; and almost all of them in late-middle age. She was caught off guard when the questions were fired at her without pause. As the baby was taken into care by one of the — apparently — well-meaning women. She was asked *exactly where* they had discovered the child. Kyra was able to give them the GPS coordinates . . . the ones she had been issued by the outlet which'd taken her on for this job.

Once the bureaucracy was through with, Panchika emerged from somewhere within the building looking flustered. It was that 'flustered' look which drew Kyra's attention more than anything else. How he looked as if he was *out* of his comfort zone. When she had first laid eyes on him, he had seemed *so* comfortable . . . with himself, with the world, with everything . . . now, though, he looked as if he had been through an ordeal.

And Kyra began the process of reconsidering her first impressions.

Had she got him all wrong?

She wasn't ready to draw that conclusion.

Just yet.

When Panchika stood before her, he wore a slight smile on his lips, but he clearly looked as if he was shaken. What Kyra had previously thought to be his *perfectly* arranged, shoulder-length hair was now somewhat ruffled. And there was a pair of dark bags beneath his eyes which she hadn't previously noted. Still, though, she couldn't deny the fine bone structure.

Or the burgeoning biceps.

"I'm sorry about this," he said, as if this was his fault.

Kyra was forced to mumble an acceptance of his apology under her breath, even though it clearly wasn't required.

"What should we do now?" he asked. "You think we should head back to the railway? You think we still have time to go through with the assignment?"

But Kyra's thoughts — as Panchika's also clearly were — remained fixed on what they'd just been through. On the baby they'd recovered from the foliage, in the middle of nowhere.

"I . . . don't know," Kyra finally replied.

To be quite honest, she hadn't given what they'd been doing previous to finding the baby a second's thought. Now that she did, though, it seemed so insignificant.

She glanced about.

To the orphanage they found themselves in.

She turned back to Panchika, a grim smile fixed on her lips. "This isn't your first time here, is it?"

Panchika breathed in deeply, causing his bulky shoulders to rise and fall. He shook his head then reached back to scratch his neck, as if ashamed. "No," he said. "That's one of the problems with my job — I often find myself photographing out-of-the-way places. And those are the places where you are most likely to come across . . . *surprises*."

Kyra looked back into Panchika's eyes. Those gorgeous, impossibly deep *black* eyes. She couldn't help it. She smiled. "The assignment on the railways can wait," she said. "The deadline's not for a week. There's plenty of time to return there. Plenty of time for us to go back."

"You want to go back with me?" Panchika flushed deeply, apparently not having had the time to check his tone of voice . . . to attempt to *conceal* his feelings.

Kyra pouted, then shrugged. She drew on another one of the tricks which she used to keep the men at bay during her day-to-day work as a journalist. "You look as if you're *solid* enough to hold a camera. Isn't half the trick keeping the damn thing straight?"

Panchika didn't seem to know how to take her comment at first. But then he saw the funny side, grinning and sniffing a laugh through his nose as he shook his head at the ground. His curtained hair bounced about on his forehead in an adorable, almost *childlike* way. When he looked back up at her, his expression had become more neutral. "I hate the fact that you've lost the whole day," he said. "I mean,

I know how important your time is — time is words, and words are *money*."

"I guess you could say the same for photographs."

Again, Panchika snuck a smile. "I guess you could."

Kyra glanced about, and then a thought struck her. She turned back to Panchika. "I was always taught — back when I first started my training — that the very best journalists can make a story out of their breakfast." She gestured to their surroundings. "This place, though, I imagine would be much easier." She shrugged. "What do you say? Should we report something on spec . . . hope that we can find someone interested enough to buy a piece on an orphanage?"

Panchika considered this for several moments, apparently unconvinced about the potential of the venture. In the end, though, he cracked a smile. Perhaps he divined her true intention of the reporting . . . or what would — at the very least — be described as her ulterior motive.

She didn't want to leave him.

Not *quite* yet.

There was something *intriguing* about him.

STORIES OF HOPE

*T*hey passed through the various rooms of the orphanage as the afternoon sun baked the building. Most of the rooms provided shelter for twenty or so children, all of them assigned a mattress in one of the three-tiered bunkbeds.

At first, Kyra didn't know rightly where to start.

The whole situation was overwhelming. There seemed *too much* to take in for her to just start *talking* to the children. But she finally caught hold of her senses.

With Panchika at her elbow, snapping away, Kyra did her best to make notes through her neural implant as she went through with the interviews. As they passed through the rooms, one of the women who ran the orphanage kept a close eye on them. It reminded Kyra of the mother wolf casting a careful eye over her pups.

The afternoon soon turned to evening, and Kyra found herself feeling at a loose end. She had gone through all the stories she possibly could, and Panchika had taken all the photographs he would need to put together a satisfying story. As the two of them descended the staircase — and into the orphanage lobby — the woman who had been watching them closely throughout their visit stopped them at the door, on their way out.

She touched Kyra on the forearm.

The woman's fingers felt rigid.

Strong.

She supposed that someone who worked here, at the orphanage, would need to have a strong grip. Some sort of a physical defence against whatever outside forces wished to harm.

The woman shifted a glance at Panchika and then turned to address Kyra. "The only reason I allowed you to come in here — to *speak* with the children — is because of him. Because I *trust* him. Is that clear?"

Kyra felt a tightness form over her chest.

Her thoughts scattered about her brain.

She finally got a hold on them.

She nodded that she did understand.

The woman continued to hold on tightly as if once she let go her influence over Kyra would be lost forever. She let Kyra go.

As Panchika and Kyra trod their way along the pavement to the car, Kyra felt a warmth ploughing through her veins. There was something — *something* — associated with Panchika . . . something which she couldn't deny.

And although the words were on the tip of her tongue, threatening to escape her lips, she couldn't quite allow them free. Indeed, when she spoke to him again, the words which came out were, "Can I give you a lift somewhere?"

Panchika remained pensive for a moment, clearly thinking the matter over. He looked back into her eyes, and Kyra felt herself beginning to melt. He smiled. And it seemed to open up a direct line into her soul. He could be her . . . *everything*.

"I was wondering if you would allow me to buy you dinner," he said, and then, apparently catching himself when what he said sounded like a 'date', he added, "I mean, so that we can discuss the job we didn't finish today — the *railway* tracks."

Kyra moved into him on impulse. Her heart hammered against her ribcage. This felt right — this felt *so* right. As she pressed herself into him — as she pushed her lips up against *his* — she felt a bolt of electricity pass through her body. An undeniable *magnetism* which drew the two of them together.

He kissed her back passionately.

When they came apart, Kyra found some semblance of wit still remained within her. "I'd like to have dinner, but only on the condition that we say *nothing* about work." She arched an eyebrow. "Is that acceptable?"

Panchika smiled. "I'm sure we can work something out."

They kissed again.

MACKENZIE

DEVASTATION STATE

*M*ackenzie Angliss's whole life surrounded her in cardboard boxes. The scruffy lettering — hastily written in black felt-tip pen — revealed the general contents of each of them: *Bathroom Stuff, Books and Music, Clothes*.

She felt the wooden bedframe digging into the underside of her thighs.

Inside she felt empty.

Just *totally* empty.

The Sydney sun shone in through the window, warming the side of her face.

She wished for rain.

There was a knock at the door of the guest room. But she didn't have the strength to reply . . . or —

perhaps — this wasn't a question of 'strength' at all. Maybe it was just a case of 'could' and 'could not'.

And she simply *could not*.

The door opened wide in any case. And the sleek, well-dressed figure of Diane Drake — her parents' lawyer, and the owner of this house — entered.

Today she had on a navy-blue trouser suit. She wore a pair of smart, matching high-heels which — Mackenzie could see from the state of the hardened-over blistered skin at her ankles — were her go-to wardrobe choice.

Diane had sleek, silver hair which brushed her shoulder blades. Despite her somewhat *severe* appearance — at least Mackenzie saw it that way — there was also a trace of kindness, a note of *tenderness* to her face. Perhaps it was her faintly rosy cheeks. The way that her jawline was curved rather than sharpened like a razor's edge. There was also the fragrance which wafted through the air. It reminded her of rose petals. From all she'd heard her parents speak about lawyers, Mackenzie was half convinced that this was all a contrived act; that Diane Drake might have mottled together these disparate traits of her appearance so as to appear more . . . *human*.

Well, if it *was* Diane's intention to pass for human then she was doing a very good job so far.

When Mackenzie had received the news of her parents' deaths, Diane had turned up at her house. Without speaking, they had gone about the mechanical act of packing up Mackenzie's possessions into boxes. Then they had loaded those boxes into Diane's car. Once Diane had locked up her home, they had set off here . . . to Diane's own house, where she assured Mackenzie that she would be welcome to stay for as long as she wished.

If Mackenzie was overwhelmed with grief surrounding her parents' death then it was accurate to say that she was *equally* overwhelmed with the kindness Diane had shown her. And she had managed to maintain that kindness even when she seemed just as thrown off by the sequence of events as Mackenzie herself was.

Diane held her arms crossed over her chest. She glanced back over her shoulder, out of the doorway she had just passed through, as if there might be a chance of escape.

Mackenzie wouldn't have blamed her for leaving.

She knew that this was an *awkward* situation.

Well — really — it was *beyond* awkward.

Mackenzie wouldn't have been surprised to find

that Diane regretted the offer she had made. Just what had she been thinking when she had said that Mackenzie could 'stay as long as she wished' ? She was surely in shock; unable to quite fathom the true significance of such an offer.

As long as she wished?

Really?

Diane looked at the tips of her shoes for a long few seconds. Then she raised her gaze to meet Mackenzie's. "I'm sorry about your parents," she said.

Mackenzie held herself very still. She had to consciously remind herself to breathe. Each one of her shuddering breaths made it seem she was fighting some epic battle . . . a battle which she was slowly losing.

Gradually, Mackenzie managed to break through her rigid, still posture to give a nod. But she still couldn't find any words.

Diane spoke again.

"If there's . . . *anything* I can do . . . you've just to let me know. Okay?"

Mackenzie measured her response then decided that she really had nothing at all to say. She managed the merest sound in reply, a half-broken, "Okay."

And — just like that — Diane turned and walked out of the room, bringing the door shut behind her.

For a long while, Mackenzie sat slumped on the end of the bed, unsure what to do. The sun continued to warm her face. But it did nothing to heat the incredible *coldness* which inhabited the inside of her chest.

She knew the tears would soon return.

FIRST STEPS

*I*t was three days later — and another dreaded *sunny* morning — when Mackenzie finally summoned the strength to leave the guestroom — *her bedroom* — behind.

The guestroom had everything she needed.

There was an ensuite bathroom.

And all her meals were dutifully brought up to her by Diane's housemaid.

Diane herself was out for the majority of the day; in court, or else consulting with clients. Mackenzie also knew that she was hard at work untangling the details and consequences of Mackenzie's parents' deaths; finding out exactly what it was that Mackenzie owned, and no doubt working on some sort of advice to her on just *what* she should do with that which she'd inherited.

It all seemed too soon — *far* too soon.

Her parents had been barely into their forties.

And now they were gone.

Mackenzie made it downstairs before she felt herself becoming light-headed. She reached for the banister, using it to keep herself steady, to regain her balance. She glanced about. Realised she had arrived to the kitchen. And that she was staring Diane's maid — Chanda — in the eye.

Chanda seemed just as spooked as Mackenzie. Her lips formed an O-shape.

Mackenzie found the strength — from *somewhere* — to not only raise a smile but to speak too. "I . . . wanted to go out in the garden."

Chanda said nothing.

Mackenzie slid back the French doors and stepped out onto the cool concrete slabs of the patio. She heard the leaves rustling in the warm breeze. The gentle scent of grass cut through the air in a pleasant manner. She could hear staccato *snip-snip-snips* coming from somewhere. Curious, she advanced in the direction of the sound.

And soon enough located its source.

It was a deeply tanned man. Or was he a *boy?*

Looking closer at him, she decided that he was about her age — nineteen, or so. He was working to prune the privet hedge which ran about the periphery of Diane's back garden. As he worked, the trimmings fell about his feet, clad in workman's boots.

Mackenzie drew in a deep breath.

Felt the fresh air fill her lungs.

The man was well muscled and had black hair.

For several moments, she was rendered hypno-tised by the way in which his muscles flexed and then relaxed with each one of his snips. He glanced at her.

She stumbled over a coiled-up hosepipe lying in the grass.

She worked to regain her former composition, reaching up to tuck a strand of her red hair behind her ear. Again, she summoned the strength to put on a smile.

And the man . . . the *boy* smiled back.

"Didn't see you there," he said.

Coming from further up north in the state, Mackenzie wasn't quite as accustomed to the jollier Sydney accent. It caught her off guard for a few moments.

Then she steadied herself.

It was so strange to think that this was the first

time she had felt anything like close to the real world ever since she had arrived here. She had been off in her own little world — absorbed by the loss of her parents. It had been easy to believe that there *was* nothing apart from her own suffering.

Nothing but the pain of her loss.

And yet ... *now* ...

The boy closed an eye as he took her in. "You a relation of Missus Drake's?"

Mackenzie considered answering in the affirmative. She wasn't sure why she considered lying, because she *wasn't* one of Diane's relatives. She was only the daughter of Diane's former clients. "No," she replied, finally, and then, deciding that she should add something more, she said, "I'm staying with her for a while."

The boy eyed her closely.

Mackenzie noted a single bead of sweat which'd seeped out of his forehead and which was beginning to run down the side of his face. Because she could think of nothing else appropriate to say, she indicated her own face.

The boy wiped his brow. He stared at his palm for a few moments, a smirk clinging to his lips. "Huh," he said. "Guess I've been working up a sweat, hey?"

All of a sudden, Mackenzie felt a tightness about her gut. She caught the sense that she shouldn't be here. That she shouldn't be doing *this* . . .

With a swift glance to the boy, she backed away, headed toward the house. As she went off — not offering an explanation — he called after her.

"Fancy telling me your name or what?"

REST AND REFLECTION

Mackenzie learned her lesson from her interaction with the gardener. She remained in her room for the next couple of days. Her isolation was only disrupted by Diane's daily visits.

Without exception, Diane would drop by to speak with her whenever she got home from a day of work. Although Diane was patient, Mackenzie was more than a little aware that Diane was attempting to push her beyond her comfort zone. She wanted her to make a habit of going outside again. On one occasion, Diane even mentioned that Mackenzie would be going back to university sooner rather than later. For some reason, it seemed an alien concept to Mackenzie, to think that she might resume some semblance of what she now saw as her *former* life.

But — then again — there seemed no reason for her *not* to go back to university. Her university was located near Sydney, after all.

It was about a week following her parents' funerals when Mackenzie received an offer from a family member to move away; to go and live with them on the north coast, in *Darwin* . . . Even though Mackenzie had given the matter some great thought, it had lightened her conscience when Diane had approached her soon after the funeral telling her that — *genuinely; hand-on-heart* — Mackenzie would always be welcome to stay with her. For as long as she needed.

And then there was the matter of university.

If Mackenzie did propose to finish up her degree then she would need to stay around Sydney in any case. In the end she turned down the offer from the family member, electing to stay with Diane.

Despite the progress which Mackenzie made in her grieving process — which was to say that she could bear to come downstairs for meals now; and could hold a perfectly reasonable conversation with Diane's maid, Chanda — she steered clear of going outside. She was worried about running into the boy again. And after she had so thoroughly embarrassed herself in their last meeting.

He must think she was *nuts*.

Of course Mackenzie told no one that often while she was up in her room, reading a book or surfing the web, she would glance out of the window and see what the boy was up to . . . if she could say nothing else for him then she could say that he was a *diligent* worker. He always seemed to be cooking up a sweat doing something or other. There was another gardener, too, the man who — Mackenzie soon discovered in the course of questioning Diane — was the boy's father. The father's name was Jack, though Mackenzie stopped short of mentioning the boy at all — let alone asking after his name — not wanting Diane to suspect anything.

But it seemed Mackenzie's conspiratorial efforts were in vain.

One day, Diane stopped her at breakfast, looked her in the eye, and, with a slight smile, said, "Why don't you ask what Gregory's doing this weekend?"

Right as Mackenzie felt herself dying a thousand little deaths over her bowl of granola — and at the same time realising that she now knew Gregory was his name — Diane continued her assault.

"Cinema? A walk in the park? It'd do you some good."

Blushing all over, Mackenzie bowed her head. She half hoped she might simply disappear. That the world might reach up and suck her down into it, absorbing her like quicksand.

A long silence dominated the breakfast table before Diane clearly decided that it was her duty to break through it.

"If you don't ask him then *I* will . . ."

And Mackenzie decided she had little choice.

RECOVERY PERIOD

$\mathcal{M}$ackenzie pulled away at the last moment.

She stared him in the eye — in those rich, dark eyes.

Greg's eyes.

"What?" he said. "What's wrong?"

Mackenzie glanced about. She was unsure quite how she had arrived here, to a small park in Coogee, Sydney.

As per Diane's suggestion, they had gone to see a film at the Randwick Ritz Cinema. Although the film itself had been forgettable — indeed Mackenzie had clean forgotten what it was about almost the second she'd stepped back into the lobby — the tension which'd crackled between the two of them certainly hadn't been.

Throughout the film, Mackenzie had waited for Greg to make some sort of a move. But he had held himself still the whole time. He hadn't so much as brushed his hand up against hers. Now, though, it was a different matter altogether.

Still without taking her hand, he had led her through a series of winding streets before bringing her here; to this *pleasant* little oasis located on the waterfront. And then, as they had been walking casually about the fountain which sat in the middle of the bushes and the well-trimmed lawn, he had suddenly stopped. Confronted her. Brought his hands up to cup her face. He had closed his eyes and moved his mouth toward hers.

Mackenzie felt a tremble pass through her body. She waited for a long moment, trying to gather herself together, wanting to get her thoughts back into some semblance of rational order. Perhaps she was reeling more from trauma than she dared to admit. Finally, she managed to find her voice. "Why did you wait until now . . . why didn't you . . . *touch* me until now . . . ?"

Greg glanced about as if there might be someone

watching on. He dropped his tone of voice. "I spoke with . . . uh, Missus Drake."

A tremor ran through Mackenzie's body.

It was almost as if Diane was here. But when she again looked around she could see no evidence for such an assumption.

Mackenzie felt a fresh strength flow through her when she looked to Greg again. "And what did she say?"

Greg winced slightly. Even despite the pained expression, Mackenzie couldn't help but stare at his tightly packed muscles. Not to mention *those* beautiful eyes.

Finally, as if after an eternity, he turned his eyes onto hers.

"She said that you've been through a lot," he said. "That I need to be *delicate* — let you have some space."

For a second, Mackenzie felt a flash of anger directed toward Diane. Although it was clear that Mackenzie was anything but in a 'good' frame of mind following the death of her parents, it seemed another thing altogether to go about telling others to 'take care' in her presence and similar sentiments. But at least it explained a great deal about Greg's behaviour this evening . . .

"So," Greg said, with a smile. "What do you reckon? How you feeling?"

Mackenzie held herself still. It *was* strange to think that there were so many conflicting feelings rushing through her.

Then, finally, she turned to him. "I feel like taking a walk on the beach."

SHORE THERAPY

One of the last places she had visited with her parents had been the beach. It was a routine of theirs — at least during the holidays when Mackenzie was home from university.

They would take a walk on the beach after dinner. That was the time when they talked about everything and nothing. Oftentimes, Mackenzie would find herself staring longingly off over the water, thinking about other countries, other cultures, and how they were seemingly so far away and yet united by the lapping oceans.

As she walked the beach with Greg, the sun setting on the horizon, he gently wrapped his fingers about hers. They removed their shoes and walked through the fine sand until the Moon emerged from behind a clump of cloud.

"Ice cream?" he asked.

Mackenzie nodded.

They headed up onto the waterfront walkway where an ice-cream van was parked.

"It's been a while since I had an ice cream," Mackenzie said.

Greg gave a nonchalant shrug. "We'll fix that soon enough."

Mackenzie opted for a pistachio cone while Greg went for lime.

As they sat on the harbour wall and ate their ice creams, dangling their legs above the gently rolling waves below, Greg told her about how he was working with his father, doing up people's gardens while he was on holiday — like her — from university. He told her he was studying mechanical engineering. It was after they'd finished their ice creams that silence descended over them.

Mackenzie felt her heart thumping gently against her ribs. It was only as she looked over the horizon, to the Moon still rising, that she realised this was probably the longest she had gone without thinking about her parents; without considering the plane crash which had killed them.

Maybe this was just what she had needed.

Some *distraction*.

And it was with this thought on her mind that she turned her attention to Greg — and to his dark, smouldering features — and she allowed herself to loosen up. She leaned into him, enjoying the wide-eyed expression smeared across his face.

And then they kissed.

To begin with, Mackenzie was soft with her kisses, not wanting to scare him away, or make him believe that she was reacting only out of fear; that she was using him as some kind of a measuring stick to see how her psychiatric recovery was going. When she was certain that he knew it was her — that it was *really* her — she kissed him harder.

And reached a hand beneath his shirt.

Felt his ripped muscles.

When she drew back, feeling somewhat breathless, she stared into his eyes. He parted his lips as if to speak, but she was too fast for him.

"Looks like we could have a *hell* of a summer together," she said.

AUTHOR'S NOTE

Thank you for taking the time to read one of my books. If you would like to hear about my latest releases you can sign up for my newsletter here: www.essiepowers.com

Thanks for reading!

Essie Powers

Before The Moon
The Lunar Lovescape Prologues